PRASE FO

Top 10 Romance of 2012, 2015, and 2016.

— BOOKLIST: THE NIGHT IS MINE, HOT POINT, HEART STRIKE

One of our favorite authors.

— RT BOOK REVIEWS

Buchman has catapulted his way to the top tier of my favorite authors.

— FRESH FICTION

A favorite author of mine. I'll read anything that carries his name, no questions asked. Meet your new favorite author!

— THE SASSY BOOKSTER, FLASH OF FIRE

M.L. Buchman is guaranteed to get me lost in a good story.

— THE READING CAFE, WAY OF THE WARRIOR: NSDQ

I love Buchman's writing. His vivid descriptions bring everything to life in an unforgettable way.

— PURE JONEL, HOT POINT

LOVE IN THE DROP ZONE

DELTA FORCE ROMANCE STORY #8

M. L. BUCHMAN

Published by Buchman Bookworks, Inc.

Receive a free Starter Library and discover more by this author at: www.mlbuchman.com

Cover images: US soldier © zabelin

SIGN UP FOR M. L. BUCHMAN'S NEWSLETTER TODAY

and receive:
Release News
Free Short Stories
a Free Starter Library

Do it today. Do it now.
www.mlbuchman.com/newsletter

Other works by M. L. Buchman:

The Night Stalkers

MAIN FLIGHT

The Night Is Mine
I Own the Dawn
Wait Until Dark
Take Over at Midnight
Light Up the Night
Bring On the Dusk
By Break of Day

WHITE HOUSE HOLIDAY

Daniel's Christmas
Frank's Independence Day
Peter's Christmas
Zachary's Christmas
Roy's Independence Day
Damien's Christmas

AND THE NAVY

Christmas at Steel Beach
Christmas at Peleliu Cove

5E

Target of the Heart
Target Lock on Love
Target of Mine

Firehawks

MAIN FLIGHT

Pure Heat
Full Blaze
Hot Point
Flash of Fire
Wild Fire

SMOKEJUMPERS

Wildfire at Dawn
Wildfire at Larch Creek
Wildfire on the Skagit

Delta Force

Target Engaged
Heart Strike
Wild Justice

Where Dreams

Where Dreams are Born
Where Dreams Reside
Where Dreams Are of Christmas
Where Dreams Unfold
Where Dreams Are Written

Eagle Cove

Return to Eagle Cove
Recipe for Eagle Cove
Longing for Eagle Cove
Keepsake for Eagle Cove

Henderson's Ranch

Nathan's Big Sky

Love Abroad

Heart of the Cotswolds: England

Dead Chef Thrillers

Swap Out!
One Chef!
Two Chef!

Deities Anonymous

Cookbook from Hell: Reheated
Saviors 101

SF/F Titles

The Nara Reaction
Monk's Maze
the Me and Elsie Chronicles

Strategies for Success (NF)

Managing Your Inner Artist/Writer
Estate Planning for Authors

1

A shadow loomed over her, blocking out the heat blast of the early morning sun striking across Fort Bragg, North Carolina's Range 37 training area. No question who it was—he blocked out everything good about the quiet morning. Even the chatty cuckoos and the dive-bomber buzz of passing hummingbirds seemed to go silent in his presence.

"Staff Sergeant Cindy Sue Chavez."

"Yes, Master Sergeant JD Ramírez?" Could the man be a more formal pain in the ass? She hated being called Cindy Sue and he damn well knew it, but it wasn't a good idea to talk back to a superior rank—not even when he was being a superior asshole.

Her mother, coming from Guadalajara, had thought Cindy Sue sounded American. But Cindy was Bangor, Maine born-and-buttered and no one in Bangor was named Cindy Sue because it was just too ridiculous—doubly so with her Mexican features and long, dark hair. Her parents had slipped across the border as two starry-eyed sixteen-year-olds seeking the American Dream. They hadn't known any better, but it still rankled. She sighed. America wasn't big on giving out guidebooks to help immigrant dreamers along the way. She should damn well write one, at least on how *not* to name your kids.

Cindy's personal mission to eradicate her middle name had been a success with most of her fellow Delta Force operators. Being a woman in Special Operations did have a few perks. Women were a rare commodity inside The Unit, as well as a reminder of home, most grunts were inclined to treat her nicely and drop the "Sue" after the fourth or tenth time she asked. A rifle butt in the gut often helped the slow learners.

She wasn't about to try that on Master Sergeant JD Ramírez whose dark eyes followed her every move. He positively relished how much she hated her extended name, but he was far too dangerous to risk attacking, at least directly. She loved Mama, so rather than indulging in a bit of matricide for giving her the name in the first place, she was leaning very strongly toward offing Master Sergeant JD Ramírez—from a safe distance.

The heat on Range 37 was already climbing toward catastrophic despite the early hour. Low trees struggled upward to either side of this section of the range. Today's training course lay along the low grassy hillside with scattered scrub and dotted with cheery flowers in yellows, blues, and purples. No hint of real shade anywhere.

Ramírez wore boots, camos, and a tight black t-shirt that had clearly been thought up for men like him. He wasn't exactly Mr. Handsome, but if it was what lay under the clothes that counted, he had Mr. Buff down. His skin had the same liquidy perfect genetic tan as hers, blemished by only a few visible battle scars that served to enhance the image. She'd never dated another Latino and—

Crap!

Some psychotic, "Cindy Sue" personality needed her head examined if she was thinking that about the master sergeant.

The fact that he was a Delta Force instructor standing on a Fort Bragg practice range—perfectly in his element—did help the image right along but she wasn't dumb enough to fall for any girlie, daydreaming trap. Master Sergeant JD Ramírez was magnificent in more than just his looks. He was a hundred percent superior *soldier.* That was what she aspired to. Which was ridiculous for a woman half his size, but it didn't matter. She'd known JD almost as long as she'd been in Delta Force and he was the finest warrior she'd never fought with. They had yet to be assigned to an action team together—merely "rubbing shoulders" in situations like this refresher training.

Ramírez still hadn't spoken, but she was going to wait him out. She wasn't even going to give him the satisfaction of looking up at him. Instead, she began preparing for the day.

His boots took a step away. Hesitated, then took another, unveiling the sunrise's full glare. None of the birdsong she'd been enjoying returned. His attitude had cleared the entire zone.

"Do me a favor," his voice was rough.

She squinted up at him. All she could see was sun dazzle, but she knew from experience that he never quite looked at her when speaking.

"What, Master Sergeant?" *Not choke you to death for being a personal thorn in my backside?* That was almost too big a favor to ask. And why was he haranguing her rather than the other seven operators sitting in the dirt and gearing up to survive today's test?

JD had been on her case since the first moment of the course. She didn't expect him to ease up just because she'd survived her first six months in Delta, hunting Indonesian pirates, but it was way past just being a "thing." His *un-*

favoritism was so blatant that the other operators had unwound from their arrogant male smugness of innate superiority enough to comment on it. None had offered to protest on her behalf, of course, but that was fine. As a Delta operator she could take care of herself.

And JD Ramírez was now topping her list of things to be taken care of. Not in a good way. She'd start by stuffing his head inside The Foo Fighters kicker drum. Then have Beyoncé strut her stuff up and down his back while wearing her gold-flecked spike-heel boots. If only.

Today was the final sniper stalking test. It was the last day of a month-long skills refresher. Not a lot of field stalking involved in hunting Indonesian sea pirates. Her shooting precision from a moving platform like a boat or helicopter had certainly been honed, but Delta didn't believe in letting *any* skills go stale. If that meant every deployment ended with a month under the ungentle thumbs of the trainers—who were fellow operators—it was fine with her.

But she was getting a real antipathy for that trainer being JD.

"Don't fuck up, Cindy Sue," he finally managed to grunt out.

"Thanks, Master Sergeant. That's *real* helpful." She didn't need advice on how to get through today's sniper stalking test—especially not from JD Ramírez. She wished she had a few rounds in her rifle to deal with him. Maybe pepper the dirt as his feet to make him dance to *her* tune.

"I'll be your spotter."

Perfect! "Yes, sergeant. Glad it'll be you." So perfect that if she had a spare live round, she just might shoot herself in the foot to get out of it. She could feel the other seven of her teammates risking glances at the friendly little tête-à-tête she was having with the master sergeant. Why wasn't he giving *them* any beef? They'd been working quietly together, preparing for the day.

In stalking tests, spotters were definitely not the helpful guy looking over your shoulder and calling out range-to-target, wind speed, temperature, and all of the other factors required in long-shot marksmanship.

She'd aced the shooting part of the course days ago.

Now, his job was to sit in the target's position with a high-powered scope and try to spot her crawling through the brush to kill him—with a single round. If he could pick her out, catch her even bending a stalk of grass the wrong way, she'd flunk the test and have to start over. Three fails and she'd be bounced back to a full week of stalker training.

In other words, not a chance was she going to let *anyone* spot her. Especially not Mr. Perfect Soldier JD Ramírez.

She continued preparing her ghillie suit. An itchy mesh of burlap and tattered string, it broke the unnatural shape of a sniper slithering toward their target. Once interwoven with local flora, it would drape like a cloak over her head and body, making her into a small patch of slow-moving landscape. An extension of the ghillie would wrap around her rifle. She began lacing in bits of foliage that were native to this particular range. New Jersey tea and sweetfern grew well here. A small selection of the summer grasses, even now shifting from flexible green to August brittle brown, would add to the suffocating layer she'd be spending the next four to five hours underneath.

There was a certain...stench to a well-prepared ghillie suit. It reeked of everywhere it had been. Dragging it along a dirt road for a 10K run had impregnated it with Fort Bragg dust and grime. Trips through reeking mangrove swamps, snorkeling across cow manure ponds, and crawling up the insides of large sewage pipes had added their own head-spinning miasma of awful.

The Marine Scout Sniper Course had a "pig pond" to teach their snipers to go through *anything* to reach the target. The Delta trainers were far less kind. The old Maine saying, "Cain't get the'a from he'a" simply wasn't in a Delta vocabulary.

Ghillie suit smell never truly washed off the skin considering the number of hours they'd spent wearing them. The scent clung until at least a couple of layers of skin had been shed over time. It worked as a high-quality male repellent in any bar—certainly better than Deet against the avaricious mosquitos of the Maine woods on her parents' farm.

The smell formed an impenetrable barrier to anyone—except for a fellow sniper. To them it was the sweet stench of belonging. However, repelling all would-be boarders wasn't much of an issue after the first day into the refresher course. Delta training schedules didn't leave much spare time in an operator's schedule. Going to the bathroom. Maybe. Eating? On occasion. Sleep? Yep, sleep was for SEALs and other lazy-ass wimps.

She sat cross-legged in the hot sun and continued working on preparing her ghillie. She did her best to ignore Master Sergeant JD Ramírez as he glared down at her.

There had been a synergy between them since the first day—an unacknowledged one. She never shot as well as she did when JD was watching her. There was something about his mere presence that drove her to be better. At first, she'd hoped that he'd eventually notice the woman inside the soldier.

After the last thirty days, she figured she could do with a lot less "notice."

2

JD did his best to look away from Cindy, but it wasn't working. He had a full, eight-operator squad that he'd been hounding through the course for thirty days. Just as planned, they now looked battered and weary. They were completely in that head-down, whatever's-next-bring-it-on mode that every Delta operator knew to their very core. The battle was mental. The course was partly a skills refresher, but mostly a reinforcement that mere human limitations weren't a part of being Delta.

At least he had seven of them in that mode.

Number Eight, Cindy Sue Chavez, sat calm and collected in the blazing sun, plucking up the local plants for her ghillie as if she was collecting a wedding bouquet. Nothing he or the other instructors had thrown at her made her fade in the slightest. Hell, *he* was exhausted.

Delta instructors didn't slack off—they were on rotation, in from field operations as well. If the squad did a mile swim wearing boots, ammo, and a heavy rifle, the instructors swam right beside them wearing the same gear. His shoulders still throbbed from yesterday's ten-mile hike with a forty-pound rucksack, just before the last test day on the shooting range—an exercise designed to rate ability to shoot after a hard infiltration. He was just glad it wasn't his day to crawl across the field hoping to god that some sharp-eyed spotter didn't pick him out of the foliage and send his sorry ass back to the start line.

"What is it about me that you hate so much, Master Sergeant?" Cindy didn't look up from preparing her ghillie suit. Her voice was a simple, matter-of-fact, want-a-soda tone.

"Hate? What makes you think I hate you, Chavez? No more than the next operator who slacks off."

It earned him a single long look from her dark brown eyes before she turned back to preparing her ghillie.

Yeah, they both knew she hadn't been slacking off and he'd been chapping her ass.

"Just don't screw up today." He walked away before he could say something even lamer.

Delta women were rare, but he'd worked with a number of them and was past being gender-biased in either direction. Except Cindy Chavez belonged in a gender all her own. Delta women were tough, real hard chargers, just like the men—Delta Force didn't recruit anyone who wasn't exceptional.

But there was something about her that blew all his calibrations about operators.

Was it her beauty? The fact that she was a top athlete? The fact that she didn't take shit from anyone—not even him? He especially liked that about her.

He hadn't even been able to think of another woman since he'd first met her over a year ago. It had certainly cut down on his favorite recreational pastime. He'd look at a bar babe with her bright blues and deep cleavage zeroed in on him, and then picture the slender, dark-eyed Cindy Chavez and he was outta there.

Even now he could feel those thoughtful, unrevealing eyes tracking him as if he was her next sniper target.

He walked over the broad, kilometer-long hillside slope that she would be crawling across. It was as ugly as a Kansas prairie—a place he hadn't been able to leave fast enough. He took his seat on the raised platform for the spotter/target—last of the three to arrive. Open to all sides, it had a wooden roof that seemed to focus the heat, even if it blocked most of the sun. From the central rafter dangled a metal target that the snipers would have to hit in order to pass—hit without being spotted.

There wasn't a breath of air. No wind to mask the sniper's traverse through the grass and brush. None that would get in his lungs after standing so close to Cindy Chavez and watch her fine-fingered quick movements of preparing her ghillie.

JD hoped that she made it, he really did. He knew he'd pushed her harder than any of the others. But his next assignment badly needed a woman of Cindy's caliber if they were going to survive it.

3

A three-hour skull-drag across the field. *Never bring your head up. Never move two inches when one would do.*

Four of the eight stalkers had been picked off by the sharp-eyed spotters. They'd have another try at it after lunch —by which time the North Carolina heat would be beyond brain-baking and their limbs would already be weary beyond functioning from their first attempt. Fine motor control would be out the window.

Not her.

A Marine Scout Sniper had to start a thousand meters out and crawl undetected to within three hundred meters from the spotter/target. A Delta operator was supposed to get within a hundred: the length of a football field from the best spotters in the business. A fifteen-second sprint away.

The first of the snipers to reach the start line undetected just fired off a blank to indicate he was ready. The three spotters on the platform all focused on finding him. She'd bet it was "Grizzly" Jones. His beard was as unruly as a bear's, which was a fair description of his body shape as well. He was incredibly good.

If the spotters couldn't find him, they'd clear him to fire a single live round at a metal target hanging over their heads. If they still couldn't find the shooter by muzzle flash, or by the blowback suppressor stirring up the grass, then he'd pass the test.

The rule was: no one else moved while they waited for a sniper's second shot.

They were unable to find the shooter. The spotters cleared him to fire.

Cindy heard the hard crack of his live round followed almost instantly by the sharp clang of the metal target mounted in the center of the spotter group.

The spotters continued their efforts, but miscalled his location by a good three meters. A sniper not only had to arrive invisibly, he was also supposed to avoid being shot immediately after making his own kill.

The sniper rose on the all clear signal. She didn't bother wasting time to see who it was.

One thing she'd learned about Delta, rules were for other people.

Since the moment everyone's attention had focused on finding Grizzly—or whoever—Cindy had been headed sideways.

4

Two more snipers had passed. That meant there was only one left and JD would be damned if he could find her.

The time limit was fast approaching and he didn't want Cindy to time out. He needed her on his next assignment. He wanted this success for her. He wanted her—

The thought petered out there. An unfinished truth.

He rubbed the sweat from his eyes. The air was shimmering at even a hundred meters. The smell of baking grass, scrub, and the unique blend that was Fort Bragg dirt—that he knew so well from crawling across so much of it himself over the years—was distracting him.

What would Cindy smell like? Not in her ghillie, but instead fresh from a shower after a hard day in the field? Or still hot and sweaty, lying back among the five-petaled wood-anemone? He liked that thought. It made a pleasant companion as he returned to scanning the field. The controls on the tripod-mounted scope nearly burned his hand with the late morning heat.

He figured it was okay to think such things, as long as he

never showed them. To keep such thoughts about her in check—which was damned hard because she was so incredible—he made a point of keeping her angry at him. Her name had been but the latest of many techniques, but already she was growing immune to it. He was running out of ploys to avoid thinking about her.

Focus on the hunt.

A sniper wasn't just a hunter who could kill at a distance, they were also a countersniper. The very best snipers hunted other snipers. Finding a sniper hunting *him* was eerie…and fun. How he'd stumbled into the best job on the planet, he didn't know. How a woman like Cindy had charged into it simply awed him. He *knew* how goddamn hard it was.

Did that stalk of yellow lupine waver with the blurring heat, or because Cindy had brushed against it? Or was it a part of her ghillie suit? He wouldn't put it past her to put a bright flower in her camouflage, simply because no one else in their right mind would think to do something so likely to draw attention.

Was the dark spot at the right edge of the field and a hundred and twenty meters out just a dark spot in the foliage, or was it the bore of Cindy's rifle aimed his way? There was no glint of the glass of her rifle scope immediately above the dark spot, so he moved on.

There was a directionless snap of someone firing a blank round.

It had to be Cindy, she was the only one left out there. He double-checked his watch. One minute inside the time limit, she was still good. Knowing her, she'd probably been in position for an hour and had simply waited to make him worry.

A glance down the line at the other two spotters. Neither one had a clue.

He felt an itch between his shoulder blades, but couldn't pin it down.

He called out, "Clear to fire."

All three of them had their heads up from their scopes hoping to spot the muzzle flash. Typically, they could pin down the shooter's location within a dozen meters before the shot, then used the scopes to pinpoint for the muzzle flash. Not this time.

Her second round slapped into the metal target. The other two trainers were still scanning the field.

JD glanced up at the battered metal target dangling over their heads and couldn't help smiling. A thousand rounds had scarred the front of the metal plate. There was only one impact splash on the *back* of the target.

He turned to look behind him. He should have trusted that itch between his shoulders.

A quick scan told him that there wasn't a chance that he was going to spot her—there was a line of dense brush behind the spotter's platform.

The other two spotters noted the direction of his gaze. Their protests about the trainee leaving the boundary of the stalking field were immediate, but he didn't bother listening.

He might not be able to see her, but Cindy Sue Chavez was exactly what he was looking for.

5

In the last twelve hours, Cindy still hadn't gotten over JD's knowing smile. It had been erased by the time she was called "clear" and had descended from an exceptionally prickly hawthorn tree she'd climbed into on the wrong side of the range.

There's been no hint of a smile as he'd ordered her to prepare for immediate deployment.

"We have an assignment," he'd addressed her without the derision that had become his standard *modus operandi* these last thirty days. "Deep infiltration. High risk. Masquerading as a couple. Minimum time is anticipated as thirty days. If it goes right, we may be deployed for several months together. You're my first choice and my only choice. We'll leave at sunset. Does that work for you?"

Deep undercover with Master Sergeant JD Ramírez? Not the pain in her ass that he'd been for the retraining, but rather the most impressive and attractive soldier she'd ever met—suddenly addressing her as an equal?

Her surprise was vaster than the hundred and thirty acres

of the Range 37 shooting range and she'd barely managed to nod her agreement.

At sunset, they'd hustled aboard a C-17 Globemaster transport jet and staked claim to the steel decking of the sloped rear ramp—one of the most comfortable spots on an uncomfortable plane. It had turned southwest toward Mexico and he had done what all Spec Ops warriors did on a flight—passed out. Headed into a mission, you never knew when you'd get to sleep next, so the jet engine's conversation-ending roar worked better than a general anesthetic on any Special Operations warrior.

Except it didn't for her this time. Maybe it was because she'd spent six months deploying from helicopters; sleeping to the heavy downbeat of the rotors while being rocked in the cradle of a racing Black Hawk was her norm. Maybe the stability of the massive C-17 is what was throwing her off.

She didn't want to think that it might be his enigmatic smile that was costing her precious sleep. She'd expected him to be pissed at her trick—the other two spotters certainly had been—not smile.

JD Ramírez was a classic Delta soldier—nothing about him stood out, at least to the untrained eye. It was the SEALs and Rangers who tended to have the big guys. A Delta had strength and skills like the other teams, but mostly they possessed an irrationally extreme perseverance against all odds. None of that showed on the outside.

While not overly handsome, that smile had completely altered her view of him. After thirty days of hounding after her to outperform every operator around her, his smile—so clear in her rifle scope—had been beyond radiant. And not as if her success was his doing; she knew *that* type of arrogance all too well.

No. It was as if he was proud of her in the way her father

had been the day she'd joined up to defend their new country.

Cindy would be damned if she was going to get all sniffly. That wasn't in a Delta's personality matrix, but she still couldn't shake that smile. It was a long time before the engine roar anesthetic kicked in even enough to doze.

6

Turning his back on where Cindy Chavez lay beside him during the flight didn't help matters in the slightest. JD couldn't believe what he'd seen as she'd crawled out of that hawthorn. Bloody from a hundred thorn scratches—and a smile as big as the sun in the Kansas sky.

He remembered the first day he'd seen her. He'd been the lead range instructor at the shooting test during Operator Selection. A hundred and twenty applicants were down to fifteen before they reached him. His goal was to make sure that every one of the fifteen was also a top marksman. By this point in the selection, a missed target wasn't a black mark, instead it was an opportunity for instruction—right up until too many misses knocked the hopeful back for retraining.

You're not reading the heat shimmer correctly.

Don't hesitate before a heartbeat, instead plan for it. At a thousand meters, the surge of blood driven into muscle by a heartbeat could shift a shooter's aim by several meters.

Of the twelve who made it through the shooting test,

there was one he never had to give a correction to, because she never missed. He'd placed her last on the second day of shooting, by which time the wind was kicking hard and gusty over the blazing pasture of the Range 37 stalking range. Undeterred, she'd finished the test with only two misses—an incredible achievement he was only able to match, not beat.

"How the hell did you do that, Cindy?" Without even thinking, he'd rolled over on the steel decking to face her. She was so close and so goddamn beautiful that he couldn't find the air to explain what he was asking about. He wasn't even sure himself anymore. They were close enough that, despite the dim red nightlight of the cargo bay, he could see every eyelash as her eyes fluttered open.

The Globemaster was transporting a pair of Black Hawks and a half dozen pallets of supplies to Colombia for the never-ending drug war. The crews and equipment crammed the eighty-by-eighteen foot bay solidly. Their vehicle—a totally incongruous Dodge Viper sports car that he couldn't wait to drive—rested on the last pallet in the line. The two of them lay on the C-17's sloped rear ramp close beside it. They'd be getting off much sooner than everyone else aboard.

She blinked at him in surprise.

"You actually talking to me, Master Sergeant?"

"Might be," not that he'd admit to it. And now he was close enough to smell her. The odors of the sniper exercise had survived her shower, but there was another, indefinable scent that almost had him reaching for her. She smelled of wilderness, adventure, and a warm fire on a cold winter night.

"Will wonders never cease," she muttered, little louder than the engine roar. "How did I do what? Climb a tree with no one noticing?"

"You did that by ignoring the rules, which is one of the reasons you're on this mission. By the way, how close were you before you did that?"

"I was inside the shoot line for twenty minutes before Grizzly shot, but once I crawled there it seemed too simple."

"Too simple," he grunted out. The stalking test was one of the hardest challenges there was for a sniper, and she'd shown a level of confidence exceptional for even a Delta by not just taking her victory.

She nodded.

"Where did you learn such patience?" He'd meant to ask where she'd learned to shoot. Her eyes skittered aside strangely at his new question. "Don't lie now. You already cheated on the test this morning. One sin per day should be enough."

Her eyes slowly returned to focus on him. Made even darker by the Globemaster's dim lighting, they seemed to reveal more of her than they ever had before. "Are you sure?"

"Am I sure of what?"

"That one sin per day is enough."

He propped his head onto his fist, with his elbow placed on the steel deck so that he could look at her more clearly. Unsure of what she was referring to, he shrugged and hoped that she'd continue on her own. The engine roar seemed to build during her continued silence until it wrapped around them like a cocoon.

Now it was her turn to shrug before speaking. "What's the real reason you've been pushing at me so hard all month? It's not gender bias. I figured that one out on my own."

"I need you for this assignment. I need a top-performing woman."

"There's your one sin for the day. Now try again, without the half-lie."

"Some day you'll have to tell me how you did that."

She shrugged maybe yes, maybe no.

JD looked at her. Really looked. They lay closer together than he'd ever been to her. As her eyes were telling him nothing, he watched her lips for some hint of her thoughts. He could just lean in and—

Get himself tossed into lockup for sexual harassment.

"I'm pushing you away because..." Because he was an idiot. He should be doing anything he could to bring her close. Though much closer and they'd be in each other's arms.

Her gaze almost skittered aside again, but this time locked and held.

"You a hypnotist too?" he barely managed to whisper.

7

Cindy wished she had a US Army Field Manual on men. JD Ramírez had been pushing her away because…he was attracted to her?

"What kind of sense does that make?"

His eyes crossed for a moment as he puzzled at her question.

"You're attracted to me?"

"No," his voice was flat, almost harsh again.

"Then *what?"*

He reached out and brushed a finger along her cheek.

It sent a chill of surprise through her so strong that she couldn't suppress the shudder.

"It's nothing as mild as that," he whispered. Then he blinked hard as if suddenly coming awake.

"Shit!"

He sat up abruptly, leaving her lying on the sloped rear ramp trying to gather her thoughts that had just scattered to the horizon faster than the big jet's turbulent wake.

He didn't go far. JD yanked off his jacket and leaned back

against the charcoal gray sports car's bumper and faced her with his knees pulled up and his elbows resting on them.

She sat up and looked at him. They were toe to toe. Beyond him she could see the 101st Airborne fliers and grunts and a couple squads of 75th Rangers. Some slept, some were joking around. There was a poker game going on in one of the helo's open cargo bays. They were all leaving the two Delta Force operators, their hot car, and their secret mission alone.

Her insides were far less orderly. Everything was tied up in knots. JD didn't hate her, which was news in itself. But he also wasn't attracted to her—it was "nothing as mild as that." What came after that was only too clear.

"You pushed me so hard so that…so that I wouldn't want to be around you?"

He nodded, then shrugged, then shook his head. But he wasn't looking up from his boots either.

"I'm a patient person, JD, but you'd better explain yourself because I suck at guessing games."

"Where did you get such patience?" He glanced up at her, looked away, appeared to realize what he was doing and finally faced her squarely.

"Change of subject."

"I asked first, and earlier."

"No way, José Domingo."

"That's not my name."

"What is it then?"

He shook his head.

She growled in frustration. "Enough shit, Jesús Dominic or whatever your name is. Speak or I'll beat the crap out of you. Right here. Right now. Faster than even any of the 75th Rangers can save you."

His smile invited her to try and she was almost tempted. When she didn't, he studied the ceiling of the

Globemaster's cargo bay for a long moment before responding.

"I've never met a woman like you, Cindy Sue," this time it was a friendly tease rather than derision.

So she only kicked his calf hard enough to make him flinch. He held up a hand to show that he'd finally gotten the message.

"The way you shoot. The way you look. Both sexy as hell." He made a point of scanning down her body.

They were both dressed in para-military-civilian-on-holiday mode: well-worn boots, cargo pants with a few too many pockets, black t-shirts, and jeans jackets. She ignored his full-body scan, because she was doing the same. Out of his jacket and frustrated past speech, he looked beyond amazing.

"But it's the way you think that truly knocks me back. I've read your entire record, probably know it better than you do I've read it so many times. You don't just think outside the box—you don't even see it. I should have known you'd hunt me from behind," he laughed with delight.

It should be irritating, but she loved the sound of his laugh.

Then he sobered abruptly. "Look. I never meant to say any of this. If you want out, we'll scrub this mission and I'll find another way in."

A sleek, late-model Dodge Viper sports car. Two Deltas posing as an adventure-seeking paramilitary couple who both looked Latino and were fluent enough in Mexican-accented Spanish to sound local. Pretending to be out of work and looking for fun in the heart of Mexico's drug country.

They were on a kingpin hunt.

Most of the cartels were personality cults run by one or two charismatic individuals. Taking out El Chapo had broken the chokehold of the Sinaloa Cartel. But others had risen in their place to take advantage of the sudden weakness. Time to infiltrate and take down some more kingpins.

It was a fantastic chance for an important and exciting assignment.

And with JD Ramírez, the best soldier she'd never served with. But what if he was more than that?

Cindy liked the way that sounded.

She liked it a lot.

"No. I'll stay." But she couldn't make it too easy on him, or his ego might get out of hand. "I think this mission sounds interesting. I like a challenge."

8

JD still couldn't get a read on what Cindy was thinking. She was not a woman who wore her thoughts on her sleeve. Or on those beautiful lips.

Her smile had either said that's all she thought the op was, an interesting challenge. Or was it some sort of double entendre about himself. He just couldn't tell. He could hope, but he couldn't tell.

Once they were seated side-by-side in the Viper—hot lady in hot car inside a combat aircraft, damn but he was doing *something* right—he reached into the miniscule glove compartment. The car's cockpit was so tight, he was practically in her lap to do so. He still didn't know if that was welcome or not, so he pulled back as fast as he could.

"Here's your ID." He handed her a battered set of Mexican papers.

She riffled them open, "Gloria Chavez."

"I thought it would be easy for you to remember to respond to because you're so freaking glorious." And he really needed to remember when to shut up.

Cindy— No! Gloria, for the duration of this mission, held the papers to her chest as if they were somehow special.

Before he could ask what she was thinking—not a chance she would tell him but he wanted to ask anyway—the loadmaster tapped on the hood of the car. Then he raised a hand as if pulling up the parking brake.

JD made sure it was raised, then gave a thumbs up.

The loadmaster began knocking loose the tie-down chains on each tire.

"What's your name?"

"I'm Juan David Ramírez on my papers."

"What's your real name?"

The loadmaster lowered the C-17 Globemaster's rear ramp. It opened to reveal the dark of night and a remote stretch of a gravel road deep in the Sonoran Province south of Nogales.

He tried to find some way to not answer the question, but couldn't find one.

He stomped down on the brake and started the car's engine. It thrummed to life. He could feel the vibration, but the redoubled roar from the jet and the open cargo bay door completely drowned the sound out.

"Jimmy Dean."

"Like the sausage?"

He sighed, "*Exactly* like the sausage. My parents wanted an American sounding name and didn't know much English when I was conceived."

Her laugh sparkled to life. She reached out a hand and rested it on his arm as if to steady herself. It was the first time they'd ever touched, other than that one stolen brush of his finger down her cheek—the softness of her skin had almost undone him there and then. She'd become a thousand times more real in that moment.

Now, with her fingers wrapped lightly around his bare forearm, energy jolted through him like lightning.

"You asked how I was so patient?" The laugh still bubbled in her voice.

"Yes?" JD responded cautiously. Now he wasn't so sure he wanted to hear her answer.

The loadmaster flashed ten fingers twice. Twenty seconds.

JD slipped the car into third gear, but kept his foot on the clutch. He hit the headlights, and the outside world leaped to visibility. Beyond the open hatch and a dozen meters below, a two-lane unpaved road raced away from them. Off to the side, lay nothing but dirt and scrub brush.

"You kept me at a distance by chapping my ass."

Cin—Gloria didn't make it a question, so he didn't do more than nod.

The loadmaster held up ten fingers. Ten seconds to go. They flew five meters above the road.

"I kept you at a distance with my patience. I made myself learn it so that I wouldn't just fall into your arms."

He risked glancing over at her. "Since when?"

Her smile was glowing. The same smile she'd worn after climbing down out of that hawthorn tree with her face all bloodied. The same smile she'd first shown him after acing the marksmanship test all the way back in Delta Selection.

"Since the first time I met you, Master Sergeant JD Ramírez. I pushed like I never had before—to get you to notice me."

"It worked. Mary Mother of God but it worked."

The loadmaster thumped on the hood and flashed three fingers at him.

Cindy locked her fingers around his arm.

The surge of joy passed into her as he dumped the brake and the car began to roll down the ramp.

The Dodge Viper gathered speed just as the steel ramp struck sparks and whirled a cloud of dust from the graveled surface.

Cindy braced for the jolt of the combat drop.

Her heart was racing, but not with the adrenaline of the tires hitting the roadway at just over a hundred miles an hour. Nor was it the deep throaty roar of the C-17 battling back aloft the instant they were unloaded to continue its journey south. The American military plane had never actually touched wheels in Mexico.

Glorious? He saw her as glorious.

He was right. It had worked. She was attracted, no, drawn to him like no one else in her life. That he felt the same was indeed a fantastic gift.

JD dropped the car into gear and, without slacking off the speed one bit, they raced off into the night. She could feel his muscles as he found the right gear for swooping over the rough road. She kept her hand on his arm because that's where it belonged.

Juan David and Gloria.

Maybe they'd just choose their names permanently, as they'd chosen their careers in Delta.

Maybe, after months of playing at being a couple, she'd choose Gloria Ramírez.

As they raced through the night toward a new adventure, she knew there was no doubt about it.

When she leaned over to kiss him on the cheek, he fishtailed hard on the gravel for a moment. Then he grinned over at her and punched it up another gear.

Together they flew down the road.

IF YOU ENJOYED THIS, YOU MIGHT ALSO ENJOY:

WILD JUSTICE

(EXCERPT)

The low hill, shadowed by banana and mango trees in the twilight of the late afternoon sun above the Venezuelan jungle, overlooked the heavily guarded camp a half mile away. But that wasn't his immediate problem.

Right now, it took everything Duane Jenkins could do to ignore the stinging sweat dripping into his eyes. Any unwarranted motion or sound might attract his target's attention before he was in position.

From two meters away, he whispered harshly.

"Who the hell are you, sister? And how did you get here?"

"Holy crap!"

He couldn't help but smile. What kind of woman said *crap* when unexpectedly facing a sniper rifle at point-blank range?

"Not your sister," she gained points for a quick recovery. "Now get that rifle out of my face, Jarhead."

Ouch! That was low. He wasn't some damned, swamp-tromping Marine. Not even ex-Marine. He was ex-75th Rangers of the US Army, now two years in Delta Force. And as an operator for The Unit—as Delta called themselves—that made him far superior to any other soldier no matter what the dudes in SEAL Team 6 thought about it. That also didn't explain who he'd just found here in *the* perfect sniper position overlooking General Raul Estevan Aguado's encampment.

It had taken him over fifteen hours to scout out this one perfect gap between the too-damn-tall trees that made up this sweaty place and, with just twenty meters to go, he'd spotted her heavily camouflaged form lying among the leaves. It had taken him another half hour to cover that distance without drawing her attention.

Where was a cold can of Coke when a guy needed one? This place was worse than Atlanta in the summer. The red earth had been driven so deep into his pores from crawling over the ground that he wondered if his skin color was permanently changed to rust red.

Why did evil bastards like Aguado have to come from such places?

More immediate problem, dude. Stay focused.

The woman's American English was accentless, sounding flat to his Southern ear. Probably from the Pacific Northwest or some other strange part of the country. But there was a thin overlay that matched her Latinate features—full-lipped with dark eyebrows and darker eyes, which was about all he could tell through her camo paint. The slight Spanish lilt shifted her to intriguingly exotic.

But she wasn't supposed to be here. No one was.

"Keeping you in my sights until I get some answers, ma'am," Duane kept his HK MSG90 A2 rifle aimed right at the bridge of her nose—a straight-through spine cutter if he had to take her down. It would be serious overkill, as the weapon was rated to lethal past eight hundred meters and they were whispering at each other from less than two meters apart. With the silencer, his weapon would be even quieter than their whispers, but he hadn't spent the last sixteen hours crawling into position to have her death cry give him away. If she so much as squawked as she went down, every goddamn bird in the jungle would light off, giving away his presence.

She sighed and nodded toward her own rifle that rested on the ground in front of her.

He shifted his focus—though not his aim—then let out a very low whistle of appreciation. A G28. Even his team hadn't gotten their hands on the latest entry into the US Army's sniper arsenal yet. Not quite the same accuracy as his own weapon but six inches shorter, several pounds lighter, and far more flexible to configure. A whole generational leap forward. Richie, his team's tech, would be geeking out right about now. The fact that he wasn't here to see it almost made Duane smile.

"A Heckler & Koch G28. What's your point, sister?" He drawled it out for Richie's sake, who'd be listening in on Duane's radio. Then the implications sank in. If his Delta Force team couldn't get these yet, then who could? Whatever else this woman was, she would be tied to one of the three US Special Mission Units: Delta, SEAL Team 6, or the combat controllers of the Air Force's 24th STS.

Or The Activity.

That fit.

The Intelligence Support Activity served the other three Special Mission Units. If she was with The Activity...that was seriously hot. It meant she was both one of the top intel specialists anywhere *and* a lethal fighter. And that meant that *she'd* been the one to put out the call that had brought him here and was sticking to see the job through. That at least answered why she was in his spot. It also said a lot that she hadn't taken any of several easier-to-reach locations that were almost as good.

"It is about time you caught a clue. Welcome to the conversation." She picked up her rifle as if his wasn't still aimed at her. Very chill. "You are being a little dense there, soldier." At least she got the *branch* of the military right this time.

"Hey, they don't call me 'The Rock' for nothing, darlin'," Duane lowered his barrel until it was pointed into the dirt. "They actually call me that becau—"

The moment his weapon was down, he suddenly was staring down the dark hole of the G28's silencer.

"Uh..."

"The Rock certainly isn't because you are a towering black movie star. It must be for your thick head."

Duane swallowed carefully, unable to shift his focus away from the barrel of her weapon to see if the safety was on or not.

"He spells his name differently. He's Dwayne 'The Rock' with a w and a y. I'm more normal, D-u-a-n-e T-h-e R-o-c-k." He made it sing-song just like the theme song from *The All-New Mickey Mouse Club* that he'd been hooked on as a little kid.

"M-o-u-s-e," she gave the appropriate response.

He couldn't help laughing, quietly, despite their positions —him still staring down the barrel of her weapon—because discovering Mickey Mouse in common in the heart of the Venezuelan jungle was just too funny.

"Normal is not what I need here," the woman sighed and there was the distinct click of her reengaging the safety on her rifle.

"Only thing normal about me is my name, ma'am." Always good to "ma'am" a woman with a sniper rifle pointed at your face.

"Prove it," she turned her weapon once more toward the camp half a kilometer away through the trees. Her motions were appropriately slow to not draw attention. However, it was too even a motion. A sniper learned to never break the pulses of nature's rhythm. She might be some hotshot intel agent—because The Activity absolutely rocked almost everything they did—but she still wasn't Delta, who rocked it all.

Duane breathed out slowly and spent the next couple minutes easing the last two meters toward her. Having the camp in view meant that one of their spotters could see them as well, if the bad guys were damned lucky. He and the woman both wore ghillie suits—that's why he'd gotten so close before he spotted her. The suits were made of open-weave cloth liberally decorated with leaves and twigs so that the two of them looked like little more than a patch of the jungle floor. He'd dragged his on backcountry jungle roads for twenty miles to make sure he smelled like the jungle as well. Having a jaguar trounce his ass wouldn't exactly brighten up his day.

Even their rifles were well camouflaged except for either end of the spotting scopes and the very tips of the barrels. If he hadn't recently been lusting over the new specs, he wouldn't have recognized her HK G28 at all in its disguise.

Getting into position as a sniper took a patience that only the most highly trained could achieve. A female sniper? That was a rare find indeed. The two women on his Delta team were damned fine shooters, but he and Chad were the snipers of the crew. A female sniper from The Activity? This just kept getting better and better. He'd pay a fair wage to know what she really looked like beneath the ghillie and all that face paint.

"Maybe you and I should go to the party as a couple." At long last he lay beside her, close enough that he would have felt her body heat if not for the smothering sauna of his ghillie suit.

"What party? And we're never going to be a couple."

"Halloween. It's only a couple weeks off. We could sneak in and nobody would see us in our ghillies. People would wonder why the punch bowls were mysteriously draining."

"And why the apples were bobbing on their own," she sounded disgusted. "What I want is—"

"Let's see what y'all are up to down there," he cut her off, just for the fun of it, and focused his rifle scope on the camp below. He was a little disappointed when there was no immediate comeback, though there was a low muttering in Spanish that he couldn't quite catch but it cheered his soul.

The general's camp was a simple affair in several ways. The enclosure was a few hundred meters across. An old-school fence of wooden stakes driven into the ground, each a small tree trunk three meters high with sharpened points upward. Not that the points mattered, because razor wire was looped along the top. Guard shacks every hundred meters—four total. The towers straddled the fence. Not a good idea. The structure should have been entirely behind the wall to protect it from attack. Unless...

"You got a name, darling?" Lying beside her, Duane could tell that she was shorter than he was. Her hands were fine, but her body was hidden by the ghillie so he couldn't read anything more about her looks.

"Yes, I have a name."

"That's nice. Always good to have yourself one of those," Duane could play that game just as well as the next person. He turned his attention to the camp. "Our friendly general isn't worried about attack from the outside or he'd have built his towers differently. He's worried about keeping people inside."

Sofia Forteza had already known that from her research, but she wondered how Duane—spelled the "normal" way—did.

She'd spent months tracking General Aguado. Cripes, she'd spent months finding him in the first place. He was a slippery *bastardo* who did most of his work through intermediaries and only rarely surfaced himself. Tracing him to this corner of the Guatopo National Park—so close to Caracas, the capital of Venezuela, that she'd dismissed it at first—had taken a month more.

Duane had taken one look at the place and seen...what?

He'd have built his towers differently.

She leaned back to her own scope and inspected them again. It took a moment to bring the towers into focus because her nerves were still zinging as if she'd been electrocuted. Somehow, in all her training, she'd never looked down the barrel of a rifle or even a handgun at point blank range—perhaps the scariest thing she'd ever seen.

Scariest other than Duane's cold blue eyes. He was the most dangerous-looking man she'd ever met, which is why his jokes and his smooth Southern accent were throwing her so badly. He sounded half badass, macho-bastard Unit operator and half southern gentleman. It was the strangest combination she'd ever heard. One moment he was wooing her with warm tones, obviously without a clue of how to woo a woman, and the next he was being pure Army grunt with a vocabulary to match. She simply couldn't figure him out.

Finally she shrugged her emotions aside enough to focus her scope properly. *Stay in the jungle, not in your head.* She rebuilt it in layers. The strange silence of the wind—not a single breath of air reached the jungle floor, instead it stagnated, adding to the oppressiveness of the heat. Macaw calls alternated between chatter and screech. Monkeys screamed and shouted in the upper branches. Buzzing flies had learned to leave her alone and the silent ants were no longer creeping her out. All that was left after she canceled each of those out was the man breathing beside her and the compound of that bastard Aguado that she'd been staring at for the last twenty-four hours.

The guard towers were supported by four long, tree-trunk legs, two inside the fence and two outside. Outside! Where they were vulnerable to attack. General Aguado hadn't built a fort in the depths of a national park—he'd built a prison.

All of her research had only uncovered his location, not his purpose here. Because she hadn't cared. Cutting the head off the snake one target at a time worked for her.

She looked again at the camp. Wooden shacks for the most part—workers' cabins. What else had she missed?

"Locks on the doors," Duane answered the question she hadn't asked in a whisper that was surprisingly soft for such a deep voice. He ignored a fer-de-lance pit viper as it slid up and over the ghillie covering his rifle barrel, slowing to inspect them with a flick of its tongue before continuing on its way in search of mice. If he could ignore the snake, so could she. Mostly. A little. She watched long after it had slithered out of sight.

Sofia looked at the shacks' doors again. Locks on the *outside*. She'd been watching the camp for twenty-four hours and had missed that. The dozens of armed guards weren't being lazy on patrol as she'd thought. They didn't care about the outside world—they were worried about the inside one. And because they were the only armed personnel in the camp, and everyone knew it, they could afford to be nonchalant.

Back to the towers. The guards were leaning on the inside rails looking down, not the outside ones looking out. All of her work to slip into this position was probably meaningless. If Duane was right, she could walk right up and knock on the front gate before anyone would pay her the least attention. A band of red howler monkeys working their way noisily through the jungle canopy above the camp didn't even attract a glance from the guards.

Still, Aguado was here. She'd seen him arrive with his entourage. And he was never going to leave. Not alive.

"Not a nice place," Duane observed quietly.

"Not a nice man."

"Sure I am. You just don't know me yet, sugar."

Sofia brought her knee up sharply. Lying side by side, she was able to bullseye the Charlie-horse nerve cluster on his outer thigh. Her nana hadn't raised her to be a target.

"Shit!" He didn't sound so almighty pleased with himself any longer, though he did manage to keep it to a whisper as he continued swearing.

Why did guys always think they were so charming? With her looks, she should be used to it by now. Except her looks were hidden by the ghillie suit. What had kicked Duane-spelled-the-normal-way into such a guy mode? Just that she was female? When did Delta start recruiting cavemen as their standard? Actually, that one she knew the answer to—since Day One if past experience meant anything.

She hadn't ever deployed with Delta before, but she'd met enough of them to know the type. They were the rebel super-warriors of the US military. Everyone thought that their team was the baddest, but Delta Force, more commonly called "The Unit," completely owned that title. Somehow they drew the people that didn't fit anywhere else in the military. But where they'd been troublemakers in their old units, 1st Special Forces Operational Detachment-Delta collected them and honed their skills. They were like a barely controlled reaction just bubbling along, waiting for an excuse to explode.

"So, what's the general's story?" Duane, once he was done nursing his thigh, went for a subject change proving he wasn't stupid.

"Deep in the drug trade. Known to have called for at least three high profile murders, including a Supreme Tribunal of Justice judge (that's their version of the Supreme Court) even if he didn't pull the trigger himself."

"Oh, so *he's* the one that's not nice," as if Duane only now was figuring that out.

She was not going to be charmed by him. His every tone said that just because she was female, he'd switched into some weird-ass flirt mode. She'd had enough of that coming up through the ranks to last a lifetime.

"This isn't slave labor, so you'd better add human trafficking to your list." With the speed of a light switch, all the charm was gone from Duane's voice.

As if to prove his point, at that moment a couple of guards exited a small building, readjusting their pants and laughing. They kicked the door shut behind them and snapped the lock closed. No question what they'd just been doing to some poor women—one of the perks of their job.

Numerous guards. Locks on the outside of the cabin doors. No large central building that might be an illicit drug lab or slave labor textile sweatshop. This was a holding pen, hidden deep in the jungle of a national park. The few people who were circulating around, aside from the guards, were almost all women. Women who were keeping their heads down and trudging about their tasks. The sickness that twisted in her stomach had nothing to do with lying still for the last twenty-four hours.

Sofia wasn't even aware of raising her rifle until Duane reached over and casually pushed it back down.

"Not yet." It was all he said, but she could hear the anger beneath the soft words.

Well that wasn't shit compared to what *she* was feeling at the moment. This place needed to be erased from the map. Scorched to the ground, removed permanently from existence!

"Why are you here? I sent for a goddamn team, not some Southern Rock."

He flashed a smile at her, "If you've got me, you don't need a team." All of his macho bravado was back. As if she'd misheard his momentary anger. He sounded too much like her useless brother and the rest of her useless family. She couldn't be rid of him fast enough.

As the last of the sunlight faded from the sky and the bird calls tapered toward silence, Sofia wondered who she was going to want to shoot more by sunrise: General Raul Estevan Aguado or Duane The Rock?

Available at fine retailers everywhere!
Wild Justice

ABOUT THE AUTHOR

M.L. Buchman started the first of, what is now over 50 novels and as many short stories, while flying from South Korea to ride his bicycle across the Australian Outback. Part of a solo around the world trip that ultimately launched his writing career.

All three of his military romantic suspense series—The Night Stalkers, Firehawks, and Delta Force—have had a title named "Top 10 Romance of the Year" by the American Library Association's *Booklist.* NPR and Barnes & Noble have named other titles "Top 5 Romance of the Year." In 2016 he was a finalist for Romance Writers of America prestigious RITA award. He also writes: contemporary romance, thrillers, and fantasy.

Past lives include: years as a project manager, rebuilding and single-handing a fifty-foot sailboat, both flying and jumping out of airplanes, and he has designed and built two houses. He is now making his living as a full-time writer on the Oregon Coast with his beloved wife and is constantly amazed at what you can do with a degree in Geophysics. You may keep up with his writing and receive a free starter e-library by subscribing to his newsletter at: www.mlbuchman.com

Join the conversation:

www.mlbuchman.com

Other works by M. L. Buchman:

The Night Stalkers

MAIN FLIGHT

The Night Is Mine
I Own the Dawn
Wait Until Dark
Take Over at Midnight
Light Up the Night
Bring On the Dusk
By Break of Day

WHITE HOUSE HOLIDAY

Daniel's Christmas
Frank's Independence Day
Peter's Christmas
Zachary's Christmas
Roy's Independence Day
Damien's Christmas

AND THE NAVY

Christmas at Steel Beach
Christmas at Peleliu Cove

5E

Target of the Heart
Target Lock on Love
Target of Mine

Firehawks

MAIN FLIGHT

Pure Heat
Full Blaze
Hot Point
Flash of Fire
Wild Fire

SMOKEJUMPERS

Wildfire at Dawn
Wildfire at Larch Creek
Wildfire on the Skagit

Delta Force

Target Engaged
Heart Strike
Wild Justice

Where Dreams

Where Dreams are Born
Where Dreams Reside
Where Dreams Are of Christmas
Where Dreams Unfold
Where Dreams Are Written

Eagle Cove

Return to Eagle Cove
Recipe for Eagle Cove
Longing for Eagle Cove
Keepsake for Eagle Cove

Henderson's Ranch

Nathan's Big Sky

Love Abroad

Heart of the Cotswolds: England

Dead Chef Thrillers

Swap Out!
One Chef!
Two Chef!

Deities Anonymous

Cookbook from Hell: Reheated
Saviors 101

SF/F Titles

The Nara Reaction
Monk's Maze
the Me and Elsie Chronicles

Strategies for Success (NF)

Managing Your Inner Artist/Writer
Estate Planning for Authors

SIGN UP FOR M. L. BUCHMAN'S NEWSLETTER TODAY

and receive:
Release News
Free Short Stories
a Free Starter Library

Do it today. Do it now.
www.mlbuchman.com/newsletter

Printed in Great Britain
by Amazon